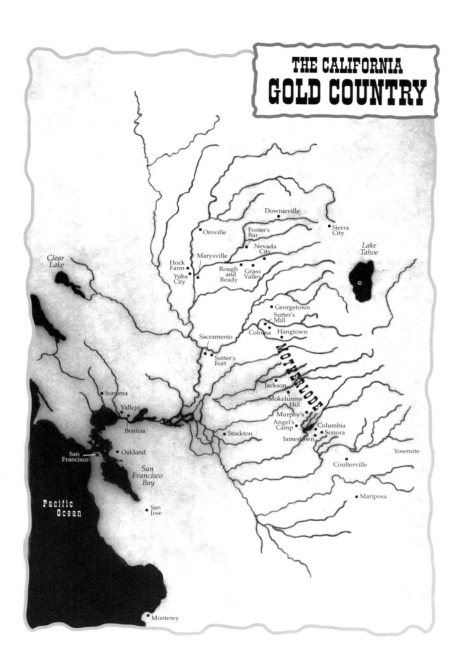

STRIKING IT RICH

Treasures From Gold Mountain

by

Debbie Leung Yamada

Illustrated by

You Shan Tang

Library of Congress Cataloging-in-Publication Data

Yamada, Debbie Leung
Striking it rich: treasures from Gold Mountain / Debbie Leung
Yamada.—1st ed.
    p. cm.
Summary: Playing hide-and-seek at their grandparents' store out-
side Oakland, two children stumble onto a secret room and letters
written by Chinese miners during the Gold Rush.
ISBN 1-879965-21-6
1.California—Gold discoveries—Juvenile Fiction. [1. California—
Gold discoveries—Fiction. 2. Gold mines and mining—Fiction. 3.
Chinese Americans—Fiction. 4. Grandparents—Fiction. 5. Space
and time—Fiction. 6. Letters—Fiction.] I. Title.

PZ7.Y18 St 2000
[Fic]—dc21
00-039190

This is a new book, written and illustrated especially for
Polychrome Publishing.
First Edition, Fall, 2001

All characters in this book are fictitious, and any resemblance to
actual persons, living or dead, is purely coincidental.

Designed, produced and published by
Polychrome Publishing Corporation
4509 North Francisco Avenue
Chicago, Illinois 60625-3808
(773) 478-4455 Fax: (773) 478-0786

Editorial Director: Sandra S. Yamate
Production Coordinator: Brian M. Witkowski
Art Director: Jeanne Wang

Printed in China
By O.G. Printing Productions Ltd.
10 9 8 7 6 5 4 3

ISBN 1-879965-21-6

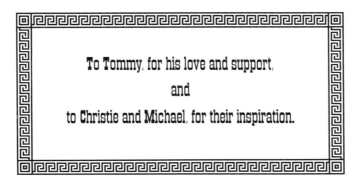

To Tommy, for his love and support,

and

to Christie and Michael, for their inspiration.

chapter 1

Summer vacation is finally here, and we're visiting my grandma and grandpa up in Northern California. They own an old country store near Oakland, and my dad and mom drive up to see them at least twice a year. My 9-year-old brother, Michael, and I really enjoy visiting our grandparents because it's so pretty here and because my grammy (that's what I call my grandma sometimes) always cooks our favorite Chinese dishes -- like potstickers and char shiu baos. But we especially like their store. Grandpa said it was run by a Chinese storekeeper in the early 1850's, during the California gold rush. But you know how grandpas can talk. If that were true, the store would be over 150 years old!

Grandpa also told us that there might be gold dust or even tiny gold nuggets that may have fallen in the cracks of the old wooden floor. If Grandpa would let him, Michael would love to crawl under the store in search of treasure. Grandpa is always teasing us, but sometimes I do wonder if there is gold under my feet.

There are many rooms in my grandparents' house. There's the big room in front where they sell just about everything you can imagine -- mostly stuff that tourists need. Michael and I especially like the old-fashioned icebox that slides open at the top. We can have any Fudgsicle, Drumstick, or Big Stick we want. It's great! My grandparents live in the rooms behind the store, which include a huge kitchen, two large bathrooms, and three bedrooms. Daddy told me that the house wasn't always this big. Grandpa added the two back bedrooms for family visitors, like us.

Auntie Mei, who is Grandpa's aunt and our great-great-aunt, tells us the best stories about the house and the "old days." Sometimes her stories are so funny that we find ourselves rolling on the floor as tears slide down our cheeks. At other times, she speaks in a soft, low voice, makes her eyes real big, and then suddenly screams out loud as if a ghost has just appeared above our shoulders. She loves to tease and scare us. Most times we aren't quite sure if she makes these stories up, or if they are really true.

There's one especially creepy story that is our favorite, and each time we visit we beg Auntie Mei to tell it. According to Auntie Mei, when she was very young, she heard that Grandma and Grandpa's old store had a secret room. From her grandfather she had learned that a Chinese storekeeper had been lynched by an angry mob of white miners in this very store. She explained that life was very hard for the Chinese immigrants during the California Gold Rush. People regarded them as too different, as odd. They disrespected them, beating them badly, and sometimes even killing them just because they were Chinese. Since this man had met such a violent death, his friends -- for he had no family here -- superstitiously boarded up the room to guard against bad luck and closed the store down. Later, another merchant took over the store and the hidden room was forgotten. It wasn't until many years later that Grandpa and Grandma took over the property from a distant relative.

Each time Auntie Mei tells us this story, Grandpa always says, "Well, if they haven't found the room by now, it's probably one of Auntie Mei's made-up stories. You know how she loves to spook you two into believing that this old store is haunted."

Each time we visit, Michael and I hunt for the

secret room, but, of course, we have never found anything . . . until this visit.

When it happened, Mom and Dad were out running errands and Grammy and Grandpa were working outside in their vegetable garden.

Michael and I were playing hide and seek. Michael was counting to 100, as usual a little too quickly. I slipped into the hallway closet -- the biggest closet I have ever seen. When we were younger, we would play house in it because there was so much room. Boy, Grammy sure does keep a lot of stuff in here.

I didn't want to make it too easy for Michael, so I balanced myself on some boxes while hiding behind jackets and sweaters and trying to hold onto the clothes bar. I figured if he opened the closet door, I'd push my feet up against the back wall so he wouldn't see me. I thought it was the perfect plan -- he'd never find me!

I held my breath as I heard Michael's zoris flip-flopping down the hall, with each step, he came closer and closer to Grammy's closet door. The doorknob creaked as he turned it. When the door opened,

I ducked as the bright light from the outside streamed into the closet.

"Christie, I know you're in here." I could feel his eyes searching around the closet. He continued to survey the cluttered space.

I smiled to myself, but my hands were beginning to sweat. I felt them slipping off the clothes bar, and my feet began losing their grip on the back wall. I had to do something fast, so I pushed as hard as I could against the wall. I wanted to jump out of the closet and give Michael the scare of his life, but in the split second before I could execute my jump, I heard a loud cracking noise, and . . . "Ouch!" I found myself under a pile of sweaters that had fallen down with me on top of Grammy's boots and high-heeled shoes.   As I flung the sleeve of Grammy's favorite white sweater off my face, I heard Michael's gloating giggles.

"Go ahead and laugh, but I really gave you a scare, didn't I," I said, glaring at his grinning face.

"C'mon, Christie, I found you, now it's my turn to hide."

"I've got to clean up this stuff before Grammy sees this mess." I got up slowly. "Did you hear that breaking sound, kind of like wood cracking?"

"Nope," Michael, still grinning, shakes his head. "Just the noise you made when you hit the floor. You're going to be in big trouble."

"Uh-oh! I think I might have broken something back here." I squeezed behind the remaining jackets. For some reason, maybe because of the impact of my fall, I wasn't too surprised to see a big hole in the wooden panel. The cool air in the closet always made me shiver, but now I could feel even colder air filtering through the hole. I reached into the crack I had just made, fully expecting a wall, but my hand went right through it.

"Michael, come here! Look at this!" But as I turn around, I see that he is gone. Shrugging, I reach for the flashlight on the shelf and shine it in the direction of the back wall. As I move the little spotlight around, I can't believe my eyes. It's a room, a really small room, but I can see a desk, some shelves, and a chair. Could this be THE room . . . the one in Auntie Mei's stories?

My heart races inside of me and I half expect to see a skeleton hanging from the ceiling. I hear Grandpa coming down the hall. "Christie, are you okay? What are you doing in there?" As I turn around with the flashlight, Grandpa stares at me from the doorway. "Grandpa, there's something back here. It's the . . . THE room!"

"What are you talking about Christie?" I quickly tell him what has happened. He didn't seem too angry with me, but he did have the strangest look on his face. Finally, he says in a quiet whisper, "Then it is true."

"Yes, Grandpa, Auntie Mei's story is true!"

Grandpa went to get his tools. I quickly pull the rest of the jackets and sweaters off the rack, while pushing the storage and shoeboxes out into the hall-way. Grandpa returns to survey the closet with a flashlight. "It looks like this closet was actually part of the original office. That storekeeper's friends were real smart. They did a good job covering up this room. I can't believe we were fooled all these years."

As the last panel was knocked out, I felt goose bumps up and down my arms. It was like stepping into a time tunnel of sorts. I mean, wow, no one had seen this room since the California Gold Rush! If it wasn't right in front of me, I'm sure I wouldn't have believed it myself! Both Michael and I had learned about the California Gold Rush period back in Mrs. Cantor's fourth-grade class, and now, here I was, ready to go back in time.

Grandpa and I are speechless as we peer into this tiny musty-aired, icy cold room, now covered with cobwebs and thick layers of dust. In spite of the dust, the sparse furniture and books look orderly and neat. Large books with faded covers and yellowed pages neatly line the shelves. On the desk are sheets of paper, an ink stone, and several Chinese brushes -- just like the ones Grammy uses in her Chinese brush painting. There is even a tiny ceramic bowl for mixing the ink. Except for the dust, everything looks like it is ready to use. While of course, there is no skeleton, it is still kind of spooky because I can almost see the storekeeper sitting in his rickety old chair at his desk. As I pick up the crisp, brownish-colored sheets of paper, I see faded Chinese characters and English letters printed on the outside. I accidentally knock an old leather pouch to the floor and a few more envelopes fall out. It was a bunch of old letters!

"Phew, it stinks in here," yells Michael, as he screeches to a halt at the doorway.

"What is this place?" he asks as he tries to squeeze in between us. "What did you find, Christie?"

"Michael, it's that secret room Auntie Mei talks about! We are actually standing in the very room used by a storekeeper during the California Gold Rush, to write letters like these! Look at these letters, Grandpa! They're in Chinese. Do you think Grandma can read them?"

"Do you think they're worth a lot of money?" asks Michael, now very interested. Ever since he started collecting basketball cards, he's always thinking about dollar signs.

"You never know, Michael," I reply. "They might be worth more money than you think. These letters are a lot older than your basketball cards, so we might be rich!"

"Well, are there any bags of gold nuggets?" he asks with that greedy look in his eyes. Grandpa laughs as I run to tell Grammy what has happened.

I can tell by Grammy's face that she is just as stunned as Grandpa to find out, after all these years, that there really is a hidden room. She is just as excited as I am about finding the letters. I spread them out on the kitchen table while Grammy reaches for her reading glasses. When we studied the California Gold Rush, Grandpa had told me that many of the Chinese storekeepers would write letters for the miners who didn't know how to write, but wanted to send letters and money back to China. The people in China thought that America was a land where fortunes could be made so they called it "Gam Saan" or Gold Mountain. These had to be a batch of undelivered letters that never made it because the storekeeper had been killed and they had been lost and forgotten all these years. "Hurry, Grammy! Read one for us," I say handing her the first envelope. She carefully picks up a letter, unfolds the delicate paper, and begins reading aloud.

To My Dear Wife,

I miss you very much, and someday I will come back. Right now the work is hard, but at least I have work. Although I miss you and the family it was good for me to come here to Gam Saan. The money I send can be used to buy grain and food to feed you and the children for a few months. At least you will not have to beg on the streets, which I hear so many people are doing back home. I am glad my parents have taken you in, and that they can help you with the children. I am sorry you have to suffer so much. I trust that things can only get better because I have work here.

The mountains of Gam Saan are beautiful, and there are very tall, green trees everywhere you look. The air is cool and crisp, very different from our humid, warm air back in China. But the nights are sometimes unbearably cold, and the icy winds blow right through our cloth tents. You would laugh if you saw me in what they call "long underwear" here. It is like a pair of pants connected to a long-sleeved shirt so that it is one continuous piece that fits very snugly. I wear it under my clothes and it keeps me very warm.

There are about 40 of us in our camp. Almost everyone is from the Kwangtung Province, so at least I have people that speak the same dialect. Our cook is very skilled and does very well with what he has, but of course, I would trade it for your wonton soup any day!

The work is hard and the Chinese are only allowed to mine after a mine has been worked over. One of the men in our group used to work in the mines back in China. His advice has been invaluable. We all worked together to build a waterwheel made up of buckets and rope pulleys. It drains the water from the rivers and makes it easier to pan for gold. We have also tried damming up a stream with logs. This leaves half the riverbed bare and allows us to shovel through the earth and catch the gold particles. Unlike the warm rivers in South China, the water is freezing cold, so by the end of the day, our hands and feet are numb. But these methods have been quite successful, and all of those little pieces of gold do add up when we put all of our finds together.

When we go into town to exchange the gold for money, many of the white men can't believe that we are able to find so much in the places they left behind. Some of them become angry and throw rocks at us, and sometimes, they even spit at us. Most of the time, we just try to ignore them because we know that they have been drinking.

I hear news that many of the miners are talking about making a law to make us, the Chinese miners, pay a special tax on the gold we find. I think it is unfair. Everyone is finding their share of gold. We are working just as hard as they are, if not harder. Besides, after paying for our debts and expenses, whatever spare money we have we send back home. An extra tax will add to our burdens, but this is not our country, so I am not sure what we can do. We have heard that some groups of Chinese have *protested against these injustices but under this country's laws, we are left with few options.*

There was a rumor that a Chinese camp was raided by a gang of angry white miners. We heard that some of the Chinese miners were beaten, and although nobody was killed, the white miners took all of their gold nuggets. But we are fairly isolated up here in the mountains, so I don't think we need to worry (nor should you). We are trying to be extra careful and stay close together as a group.

I hope the children are well and are being helpful. I hope that I will be able to come home soon.

Your respectful husband,
Wong Meng

As Grammy reads this letter, an eerie feeling comes over me. It was as if Wong Meng was speaking directly to me. How had Wong Meng come to Gam Saan? What were his wife and children like? I couldn't help wondering if he ever made it home. It was as if through these letters, I was listening to voices from the past.

chapter 2

"Will this rain ever stop?" grumbled an exhausted Wei Lin as she fell into bed beside her husband, Wong Meng. "This constant pitter-patter of rain hitting the front door, and the whistling winds sending a chill through the house has made it very hard for the children to get to sleep. I'm afraid, too, that they're getting sick again."

"They will be fine, Wei Lin. You worry too much," assured Wong Meng, as he gently put his arms around his tired, young wife. He lay back, just holding her for a minute. Her eyelids were shut, but he could tell by her breathing that she was still awake.

"Wei Lin, we need to talk about what we are going to do. The flood last week nearly wiped out our farm, and there is little for us to salvage. Although we have been living a very simple, but honest life, I am not sure we can do even that anymore."

Wei Lin's eyes were still closed, but he knew she was listening.

"I have heard," he continued, "that just last week a mob of men, with no sense of duty or principle, robbed and beat up a well-to-do farmer and his family, taking what was not theirs. What has become of our beloved China? Everyone is competing for food and work. We can't go on living like this; we need to make a change."

Wei Lin, her weariness suddenly melting away, turned and grabbed both of her husband's arms. "What," she pleaded anxiously, "are you thinking of doing, Wong Meng?"

"Listen to me, Wei Lin. I have heard that there are notices being put up around the harbors saying that Americans are rich, and they want us to come over to work the mines in Gam Saan. They promise good pay, large houses, food, clothing and spending money to spare," exclaimed Wong Meng, his voice rising enthusiastically.

"And you believe this, Wong Meng?" replied Wei Lin, mockingly. "I thought you had more sense. Well, I have heard things too. Like the story of Mei Lai, who was one of the village's first wives to let her husband go. She waited for months and months to hear from him. She was so proud, all along thinking that when her husband returned she would be a rich man's wife. Finally, she receives a letter, not from her husband, but from the village association. They said her husband got so sick on the boat that he died on the way over and never even made it to Gam Saan! Now, she's a widow with two young children and no hope. And you expect me to let you go?"

Wong Meng knew that his wife would be hard to convince, but he had been thinking about their situation for a long time. "Yes, Wei Lin, I have heard similar stories. But the chance of our entire family starving to death is just as great if I choose to stay here. If there is something I can do to prevent that, don't you think we need to take that risk? I can't stay here and watch us lose everything. Ping told me that his cousin left for Gam Saan six months ago. He just heard from him and all he wrote about was how much gold could be found. He said it is everywhere, and anyone can just pick it up out of the streams!"

There was no response from his wife.

"Can you imagine, Wei Lin? If I go to Gam Saan and find this gold, I can take care of you, my parents, and our children for the rest of our lives. I think it is worth taking the chance. The longer we put off making a decision will make it that much more difficult. Our situation is not getting any better; instead it grows worse day by day."

Wei Lin was silent for several more minutes. She knew Wong Meng was right. Life had never been easy for them; especially more so in the past year. It was hard, though, for her to imagine a life without him. If Wong Meng were to go to Gam Saan, she and the children would have to live with his parents and his brother's family. Though her small, but comfortable, house consisted of a mere two rooms for sleeping and eating, she would miss it because it was their own. She was not one to wish for riches, a house with many rooms and courtyards, or gold jewelry and silk robes. She felt she could live contentedly as long as there was enough to eat. But she could see in Wong Meng's eyes that he was determined to follow through on this dream of his.

"How," she asked quietly, "will you come up with money for boat passage?"

Wong Meng sensed a slight opening on Wei

Lin's part. "We can borrow money from my parents, my brother, and maybe even your parents. And then I can sell some of our pigs, and maybe, even that skinny, good-for-nothing water buffalo. This can be done, Wei Lin! I have thought this through for the past several months. In no time I can get the money and be on the next boat to Gam Saan."

"But you have never left home before. You have never even left the district, and now you want to go across the ocean to the unknown?" Wei Lin paused and took a deep breath. "How," she asked, her voice beginning to quiver, "will you know what to do once you get there? You're a farmer. Who will teach you how to mine?"

"Ping said it was no problem. He is ready to go and wants me to go with him. Look at how many men in our village are going. I am not the only husband who has to leave his family behind. There are more and more of our fellow countrymen going over every day."

"What about the authorities, Wong Meng? It is against the law to leave this country!" said Wei Lin, trying to appeal to his sense of duty.

"You don't need to worry about that. Those

Manchus in the North don't really concern themselves with us down here in the southern part of China. You know as well as I that the local magistrates are only interested in benefiting themselves. Why should we be at their mercy? Ping knows some people who will take care of everything if you pay them a certain amount of money. These days everyone has a price. It's happening all the time; those lazy officials just look the other way once their pockets are full.

"Once we get over to Gam Saan," continued Wong Meng, "our village association will send their representatives to meet us at the boat and make all the necessary arrangements for work and food. Ping says it will surprise you to know how very organized it is over there."

"Ping this, Ping that. I hope Ping knows what he is talking about. He doesn't have two small children like you or even a wife half as pretty as me. No wonder it's 'no problem' for him to go off to the land of foreign devils!"

"Yes, Wei Lin, you are right. Ping's wife isn't half as pretty as you," laughed Wong Meng, relieved that his wife's sense of humor was still intact. "I know you don't want me to leave, and I don't want to leave either. I shall miss you and the children more than I can tell you."

"Then why don't you take me and the children with you?" Wong Meng looked silently at his wife. She, of course, knew as well as he did, that would be impossible. It was totally against all the Confucian teachings of her upbringing. As a young girl, she had been told all too often that a woman must obey her father as a daughter, her husband as a wife, and . . . she shuddered at the thought, her eldest son as a widow. She knew it was impossible for the entire family to go with him. But she wanted to hear Wong Meng say that he would take her if he could.

"Oh, foolish wife," Wong Meng affectionately smiled at her, "if there was a way, you know I would. But your place is here at home taking care of the children and watching over my parents. Besides," he added half jokingly, "with you still here, my parents will be assured that I will not forget to send money back to China for everyone." As he looked at his wife's downcast face, he brushed away a single tear that threatened to erupt into a full cascade. "I don't think we have much choice right now. I must go. This may be the only way for us to get back on our feet. I really don't think it will take that long. In just a few years, our lives will be ten times better, I promise. You must let me do this for the future of our family. Can you understand what I am saying? I need to make my own destiny."

That night as Wei Lin lay next to Wong Meng, listening to his steady breathing, she no longer tried to stop the flood of tears from flowing down her cheeks. There were still so many more questions and doubts that raced and rearranged themselves in her mind. Could she trust that the gods would watch over her husband in a foreign land? What if Ping was wrong and there was no one on the other side to help him get started? What if Ping was wrong about everything? So many things could go wrong, yet she knew that Wong Meng was right. There was no other choice. In order for the family to survive, Wong Meng had to go. She would have to stop thinking about all the bad things that could happen and instead trust that Wong Meng, who had always been motivated and resourceful, would be strong and wise enough to cope with the challenges that lay ahead.

Yet, Wei Lin couldn't quell the uneasiness she felt in her heart. She pushed away her feeling that once she let her husband go across that ocean she would never see him again. And when she had no more tears to shed, a completely exhausted Wei Lin fell asleep.

chapter 3

"I'm sorry, Grammy, did you just say something? As you read the letter to me I felt like I was in another world; I could almost hear Wong Meng's real voice talking to his wife."

"You know, Christie, I feel the same way. It was as if ghosts from the past were speaking and their words are echoing in this very room."

"That's kind of creepy when you say it like that, Grammy!" I imagined see-through human forms, in long, flowing Chinese robes, floating in and out of the kitchen. It gave me the shivers.

"I don't mean real ghosts, Christie. It's just that because these letters were written so long ago, our reading them enables us to go back in time and see through the eyes of men such as Wong Meng. It's a very personal view of history. People were so desperate in those days that they would do whatever it took to survive. California or Gam Saan, the Gold Mountain, to them offered the only hope for a better life, and they were willing to sacrifice just about everything to get over here."

"How long did the men have to stay away from their families, Grammy, do you know?

"Well, it was probably at least 3 or 4 years and sometimes that stretched to 10 years or more. When I was a young girl in China, there was a Cantonese folk song we used to sing that went something like this:

If you have a daughter,
don't marry her to a Gold Mountain man.
Out of 10 years he will not be in bed for one.

"I didn't really understand it at the time. It wasn't until much later that I realized how very common it was for men to leave their wives and families to come over here for years and years.

"Really? I sure wouldn't like it if my dad had to go away. Sometimes he goes on a business trip for a few days and that's enough for me."

"Well, I'm sure most of them expected to return to China sooner, but it probably wasn't as easy to repay their debts as they had thought. They didn't bring their wives because the Chinese custom was that wives had to stay behind to care for their parents and children. Most parents also figured that their sons would return if they had a wife and children waiting. Later, the United States passed laws and many restrictions that made it very hard for wives to come over. There was a lot of prejudice against the Chinese and this was one way to limit their population. So even though the Chinese have always valued the family, many families were separated from each other for long periods of time. It was very sad because fathers never saw their children grow up, and couples had to live apart."

"You know, Grammy, this is like learning history, but it's not boring. Let's look at another letter."

Dear Papa and Mama,

I am writing to tell you that I have arrived safely at Gam Saan after three long months on the ship. It was a very rough trip and just about everyone got sick. I was sick most of the time, too. The constant back-and-forth motion of the boat made it hard for me to keep food in my stomach. Finally, spotting the San Francisco Bay when we were allowed on deck was a welcome sight.

It was such a relief to breathe the fresh air. I was so

happy to get off that boat; there was so little space for each person below. We felt like our pigs back home crammed into a small shed with no room to even turn around.

At the dock, a Mr. Chan, from our Huiguan Association, met us and took us to a room to sleep overnight. We ate some rice and dried fish, and it was the first time in months that I could eat until I was full. Mr. Chan told us that in a few days we would join a group of other Chinese miners and travel to the mines together.

Mama, I know you worry a lot about me. But the associations here are very organized and everything is as they told Papa it would be. There are many men who are about my age, though there are some who are older. We sleep in beds that are built one on top of another, and have been given clothing suitable for the weather and mountains we will encounter. They are preparing us to go to the mines. Mr. Chan is very helpful, and when I told him my name and village, he said he knew our Uncle Chee. I had to tell him that Uncle Chee had died because of the famine that had spread to his village just a few months before I left. He was sad to hear that yet another one of his friends had died. He asked how my family was, and I told him that you were surviving, but with difficulty.

How does the harvest look, Papa? Are Kai and Little Brother helping in the rice fields? I hope that they are not complaining too much or fighting with each other. Tell them that I miss them.

On the boat we talked of nothing else but the gold that is said to be everywhere. I half expected the roads to be covered with it. The older men would shake their heads at us and tell us that it is not as easy to find gold as we think. But I am sure that once we get started, I will be able to pay back the $70 "credit ticket" in no time. They tell me that for just an ounce of gold, you get $16! If that is true, I can pay my boat passage in no time and still have plenty to send back to you and then some.

Please do not worry yourself about me, Mama. There are a lot of "uncles" here who watch over me like family. Of course, I miss your cooking and sitting around the dinner table with all of you. Tell my little brothers that my time away will fly by quickly.

I will write again as soon as I can.

Your son,
Wing Wah

"Three months sounds like an awful long time to be cooped up on a boat. I'm sure I would get seasick. How long did it take you to come by boat, Grammy?"

"Well, I think it took about 21 days to get from Hong Kong to San Francisco. Of course, the boats in our day were a lot more comfortable and faster than back then. I had read that during the California Gold Rush, there were so many Chinese wanting to go to Gam Saan, that shipping companies would try to squeeze in as many people as they could. The more people they had, the more money they made. Sometimes, because the boats were so overcrowded, diseases would easily spread throughout the entire boat. So it was not unusual for it to arrive at the harbor with only half of the Chinese travelers alive."

"That's awful, Grammy. I guess it was a big deal then if you just made it across the ocean safely. This guy must have felt pretty lucky. Do you think Wing Wah ever got to see his parents again?" Just then, the letter slipped off of Grammy's lap and onto the floor. As I bent down to pick it up, I stared at the old and worn floor of what was now

Grammy's kitchen. It suddenly occurred to me that way before Grandma and Grandpa were even born, these letter writers actually walked on this very floor.

chapter 4

Wing Wah could barely feel his toes in the very stiff and curious looking leather boots he now wore. Mr. Lee, the storekeeper, had showed him how to string the laces through the holes of the boot and to tie them as tightly as possible. They fit snugly up his ankle, and he felt like he could barely lift his feet as he awkwardly took steps across the hollow wood floor of the store. Mr. Lee assured him that the fit was good and that even though they felt strange and clumsy now, that he would get used to them eventually. They were certainly a lot more confining than the light cotton slippers he was used to wearing back home. But Mr. Lee told him that Chinese shoes wouldn't last a week when working in the mines.

All the Chinese came to Mr. Lee's store for whatever food or supplies they needed. His shelves were stocked with every imaginable tool, pots and pans, clothes, hats, and even Chinese pills and herbs. There were also ceramic jars filled with salted vegetables and pickled ginger from back home. As Wing Wah looked around, he could tell that the customers came here for more than just food and dry goods.

Mr. Lee, an elderly gentleman who spoke patiently and kindly to all the newcomers, gave them much needed advice. He greeted all of his customers by name and never failed to offer them his hot oolong tea. Because Mr. Lee was a learned man, everyone came to him so he could hand write their letters and documents. While drinking tea together, he would inform the Chinese sojourners of news and events from back home. Wing Wah could tell that Mr. Lee was an important and trusted liaison to the miners and their families across the vast ocean. He felt immediately that he could trust him, too.

"Hey, Wing Wah, it's good to see you out today." Wing Wah turned to see Mr. Chan, the man who had met them at the boat when they had first arrived.

"You seem to have recovered from your long journey. Your skin color has returned and you look almost normal. When I saw you coming down the gangplank off the boat, your face was the color of a jade pendant," chuckled Mr. Chan.

"Thank you for the compliment, Mr. Chan. If I looked as bad as I felt a few days ago coming off the boat, I must have been a pitiful sight indeed. Even though I felt like I was going to faint, I was so happy to finally plant my feet on solid ground. Actually, did you see Han Low? He did pass out, right in front of me! When I bent down to see if he was all right, I found myself eyeball to eyeball with a man with two queues hanging from the sides of his ears. His looked at me curiously as I stared back at him. When he gently lifted Han Low's head and pulled out a small pouch filled with what looked like crushed leaves, Han Low responded. Whatever was in that little bag must have been pretty powerful because he perked up almost immediately and was then surprised to find himself in the arms of this strange man. The man just smiled at him and helped him up. He wasn't a Han, though he kind of reminded me of old Mr. Tong from back home."

"Oh, you must have met good ol' White Horse, or Charlie, the Indian," said Mr. Chan.

"What did you call him?" asked Wing Wah

with a puzzled look, "White what?"

"That probably was White Horse, or Charlie. He goes by either name. He is what they call an Indian," explained Mr. Chan. "As I understand it, the Indians and the Mexicans, those dark-skinned men you saw on the dock, were in this country long before the white man came."

Mr. Chan, thought Wing Wah, certainly seemed to know a lot about this strange, new world. There were so many different things to see, especially different were these white men. "So where do the white men with the flaming red or golden hair come from?" asked Wing Wah. "Their hair not only grows on top of their heads but on their faces and arms as well. They are like giants with thundering voices, and their large piercing eyes resemble the colors of the ocean. I can still hear their strange words echoing in my ears."

"All these men are here for the same reason as you, to find gold. They have traveled many miles too, across a different ocean. They are not all from the same country, but from many different countries. Most of them have a common language, which is called English. I have learned a little English myself. If you can, you must try to learn a little because it will be helpful to you while you are here in Gam Saan," Mr. Chan advised.

"I don't know if I could ever learn it. It sounds so different from our native tongue. Were some of them making fun of us, Mr. Chan? I don't know what they were saying, but their expressions did not seem as kind as those of White Horse."

"Well, you will meet all kinds of men here. Some of them are very accepting of us. Others feel that everything about us is odd to them: what we wear, what we eat, and how we look. They don't understand why we wear our queues, and many of them will pull them disrespectfully. It is hard to explain to them that if we cut them off, we cannot return home for fear of punishment from the ruling Manchus. They don't understand our ways. They don't understand, for example, the importance of making sure our associations send our bones back to the homeland if we die here. By the way, Wing Wah, you did sign all the necessary papers for yourself with Mr. Lee, right?"

"Oh, yes, Mr. Chan. I just finished having a

letter written to my parents and then I signed the forms that Mr. Lee drew up regarding my remains. Before I left, my father told me repeatedly to be sure to make those arrangements as soon as I arrived, in case any misfortune befell me here in Gam Saan. He told me that if I died in this foreign land, my soul would wander in darkness, and my spirit would find no peace in this unknown country."

"That is very true, Wing Wah. You are wise to have listened to your father. The association is very good about carrying out the requests of the dead. Rest assured that your bones will be sent home for proper burial and honored by your family if any such unfortunate events should happen to you. But it is bad luck to say any more about misfortune. I'm glad you wrote your parents right away to tell them you had arrived safely."

"I knew they would want to hear from me as soon as I got here. My mother worries. She was so upset when I left. I've never seen her cry so much. Sometimes I think she still sees me as a small child, but I'm 16 and I can take care of myself. It wasn't easy to come up with such a large amount of money for the credit ticket. My father, though, felt that in the long run, my going to Gam Saan would help the entire family in these hard times. I want to make them both proud of me, so I am determined to work hard."

"Most mothers have a hard time letting their sons come here," acknowledged Mr. Chan with a knowing glance. "It's natural for them to be concerned." He watched Wing Wah, strutting past the shelves of canned foods with a mining pan on his head and a basket full of cans and little bags.

"Well, I dream of the day I return to my village, dressed in my finest robe and hat, bearing more gifts than I can hold for family and friends. Everyone will be lined up on the streets to greet the eldest son of Wu, returning from Gam Saan with enough money to buy the largest plot of land for the Wu family. I'll have a big feast for the entire village. There will be the biggest roast pig you've ever seen in your life, and the sweetest cakes and delicacies to fill everyone's bellies as we celebrate my good fortune!"

Mr. Chan could not help but laugh out loud at Wing Wah's exotic "pan" hat, and his wonderful description of his glorious homecoming day. He admired the enthusiasm and optimism of this bold, young man, and said encouragingly, "That is what we all look forward to, Wing Wah. You will soon learn, though, that mining is hard work. The fact that you survived the boat ride across the ocean shows that you have the stamina and strength it will take to withstand the hardships of this new land. Your youth will serve you well. Do you think you have everything you were supposed to get?"

"I think I have just about everything. Let's see, I have the gold mining pan . . . didn't it make a most elegant hat? I have the pickax, knife, pot for cooking, lamp, and how do you like these strange and heavy boots? Oh, yes, I can't forget my precious rice and tea. I have to have them with me; I can't live without them."

"Well, it sounds like you are all set, Wing Wah. Let's settle the bill with Mr. Lee. I have just a few more words of advice. Stick close to your countrymen and you will have a better chance of surviving. Be warned, my son, that there are good men, and there are bad men. Most will treat you as equals, or at least with some respect, but others will not. Don't lose heart; you have every right to be here. Keep dreaming, be patient, work hard, and bring honor to your parents and our people."

As Mr. Chan turned and walked out of the store, Wing Wah thought about their conversation. He had crossed 7,000 miles of ocean in three months' time, but that was just the first barrier he'd withstood in pursuing his goal. In this new world there would be many more barriers, of a different sort to cross, before he could ever know the reality of his dreams to return home as a rich man.

He gathered up his newly purchased supplies, placed them in his straw baskets, and carefully balanced them on a pole across his shoulders. His initial enthusiasm and anticipation of the gold that would be his was tempered by the weight of all the unknowns that lay before him.

He had to admit there was a part of him that was afraid. The lingering images of the towering, golden- and red-bearded men, along with the strange sights of a new country and the deafening sounds that greeted him when he disembarked from the ship, made him shudder even now. For the past few days he had felt relatively safe and secure among his fellow countrymen. But he knew that once he left this "Little China" for his mining camp, he would be leaving all that was familiar.

Many questions raced through his mind. Questions that even Mr. Chan could not answer. These questions could only be answered with time and the experiences that lay ahead. Would he be strong enough to do the backbreaking work of mining, day in and day out? Should he worry about the golden- and red-bearded giants? What unknown obstacles or dangers would he have to overcome? And most importantly, would he succeed?

Wing Wah hoped that he had not made a mistake by traveling to this land of dreams. But he reminded himself that he was here for the survival of his family, and that Gam Saan was, at this point, their only hope.

As he stepped out the door of Mr. Lee's dimly lit store into the blinding sunlight, Wing

Wah vowed, in his inner soul, that he would do everything in his power to endure whatever hardships came his way. He was determined to bring prosperity and honor to his parents and himself.

chapter 5

Handing Wing Wah's letter back to Grammy, I saw Michael peering at another letter.

"Here, Grammy, read this one!"

Grammy studied the letter and began to read:

To My Dear Young Son, Kai Ming,

I am sorry that I am missing the celebration of your eighth birthday. You are growing up so quickly. How tall are you now? Even though I cannot be with you, I am sending your mama money to buy you some special treats like your favorite ginger candy or those sweet and salty dried plum seeds that you and I love so much. I wish we were eating some together right now.

I know that I have been away for a long time. I enjoyed reading the letter from you and your mother. I don't know if I can answer all of your questions. But, yes, we have recently found a mine that was left behind by the white miners after they worked it over. These abandoned mines are the only kind that we are permitted to work on since we are considered temporary workers in this country. We have found that there is quite a bit of gold as we dig deeper, but it is hard work. Sometimes we succeed in finding as much gold as they did the first time around, and this makes them very angry. Can you believe that they throw us leftovers, and then are furious when we feast on them? I guess that is the disadvantage of being a stranger in this land.

The white miners are not all bad. Most of the time they leave us alone, but we do try and stay out of their way. I don't want you to worry though. There are many of us; it's much safer in large groups. Actually, I am very grateful for the other Chinese men who I can talk to here. I have gotten to know several of them. We all share the same dream of finding enough gold to pay off our debts, with interest, and return home to our families as wealthy men.

Our mining camp has two cooks who have managed to keep us well fed with the foods to which we're accustomed. They are both quite masterful at taking the dried ingredients imported from home and coming up with delicious dishes. After a grueling day of mining, we all look forward to our evening meals. Occasionally, we even get a treat when they catch fish in the streams; then we have black bean steamed fish for dinner.

After we eat, despite our exhaustion, we sit together and tell each other stories. Some are stories I remember hearing as a child, and they make me homesick. Sometimes we play games that the white miners have taught us, such as "checkers" and "chess." When I come home, I will teach these games to you and your sister. I know you will not only enjoy them, but in no time you will be better at them than I am!

My good friend, Ning Yang, plays his "siu" for us. It is truly music to my ears to hear the lovely notes of his flute in the quiet night. You would like him. I told him I would introduce him to your Auntie Yee Yee. I think they would be a perfect match. He is a hard worker, and he can make anyone laugh. He and these other men are almost like family to me, and we keep each other company.

Yes, it is very beautiful here. You would especially like the tall green trees with prickly needles. The climate is a little colder than home because we are up in the mountains. Sometimes, we hear coyotes howling at the moon. I have seen them during the day. They are like large dogs, but smaller than wolves, and they run very fast. I have heard that there are bears, but I have never seen one and hope that I never do!

I miss you all very much. I hope that you are obedient to your mother and not fighting too much with your little sister. Be helpful and do your chores. It will not be long before I return home. While I am away, you are the man of the house. Be patient. I am hoping I can return in just three years' time.

> *With much affection,*
> *Your Papa, Chi Wei*

"Grammy, why are Chinese names so weird?" asks Michael curiously. "They all have funny sounds like "ying," "yong," or "wah.""

"Well, Michael, they might sound odd or funny to you because they are in a different language. In the Chinese language, all the sounds have different meanings. To make it even more confusing, depending on what part of China you were from, even though the written word is the same, the "sound" may sound slightly or entirely different. There are many different dialects or languages spoken in China. In Southern China, where most of the Chinese miners who came to Gam Saan were from, there is the greatest diversity of dialects. Most of these earliest Chinese spoke Taishan or Cantonese dialects. Language, you see, was used by the early Chinese emperors to unify new areas of conquest. Just as the Romans transmitted Latin to France and Spain, early Chinese was taken south and east by the Qin and Han dynasties, developing into Mandarin, Hakka, Cantonese, and others. The Chinese rulers were clever. As they expanded their territories, they insisted that there was only one language, Chinese, and these 'dialects' were treated as regional speech – even though they may sound as different as French from Italian.

"Then how do Chinese from different places understand each other?" I ask.

"If they can read, it's all the same script or characters. It doesn't matter if all Chinese don't speak the same dialect. The best way I can explain it would be like someone from Georgia who speaks English very differently than someone from California or even England. They can still read and write the same books and newspapers."

"I'm confused, Grammy," moans Michael.

"I know, Michael, it's hard for me to explain it,

but, let's go back to your question about Chinese names. Names in many cultures are very important, and the Chinese are no exception. Chinese names, unlike Western names, are made up of just three words or sounds, and a person's last name come first. For example, this writer's name is 'Chi Wei,' and his last name is 'Lee.' His full name would be 'Lee Chi Wei.' Now 'Chi' is his middle name, also known as his generational name. So all his brothers would have 'Chi' in their name. Then finally, there is his first name, which is 'Wei.'

"So what do those sounds mean, Grammy?" asked Christie.

"Well, his parents probably chose 'Chi Wei,' because in the Chinese language it sounds nice together and its meaning is 'great ambition.' It is very important to Chinese parents that the words that make up a name reflect certain characteristics that they hope their child will have. Some of the more popular Chinese names would have something to do with strength, intelligence, or beauty. But isn't it interesting that here is a man whose name is 'great ambition,' and he's found his way to America to seek his fortune? I know it can be confusing and odd-sounding to you, Michael, but back in Chi Wei's day, the Chinese language was very peculiar to Western ears. Sometimes they would call all Chinese men 'John Chinaman' no matter what their names were. Or they would call the women 'China Mary' because they didn't want to bother with their given names. What was worse, though, was when they made up insulting names to be mean or cruel, such as 'Ching Chong Chinaman.'"

chapter 6

"Hey you, Chink, Chink Chinaman! I know you can hear me! Go back to where you came from and stay out of our claims! Keep running, you celestial codfish, because we're gonna string you up by your lady's braid!"

"Aii…Yah!"

"Chi Wei, wake up! You're having a nightmare again. Look, you're all wet from your perspiration."

Chi Wei opened his eyes and found himself back in familiar surroundings, lying on his cot under the white canvas tent that he shared with seven other Chinese miners. His good friend, Ning Yang, had shaken him from his sleep and was looking at him with a concerned expression on his face. Inside his chest, Chi Wei felt his heart beating so fast, that he thought it would pop out. His dream had been so real. He was exhausted from it, as if he had actually run long and hard, and only now could he catch his breath.

"Yes, Ning Yang, I guess it was a nightmare, but it felt so real. Two men were chasing us and throwing mud clods. They were drunk with whiskey and were yelling and calling us names while trying to get a hold of my queue. I was running for my life. I thought that if they caught up with us, they would surely string us up with a rope, or beat us to death," chattered Chi Wei hysterically.

"Calm down, Chi Wei, it was just a dream. At least they weren't shooting bullets at your boots! And by the way, was I running in front of you or behind you?" asked Ning Yang teasingly.

"Thank you for your considerate concern, Ning Yang. You are a true friend," Chi Wei sarcastically responded. "I know I can always count on you to make a joke of things. But seriously, do you ever fear for your life here in Gam Saan? I mean, say we take all the gold in this mine we're working back to town to exchange it for money. What if we find ourselves surrounded by a mob of angry white miners bent on beating us up for our gold?"

"Hold on, Chi Wei. It was just a dream. And besides, the angry mob scene you've described doesn't happen that often. Chinese miners gamble their earnings and lose more at the fan-tan tables to other Chinese than to irate mobs."

"Yes, but you've heard the same rumors that I've heard, and even though I write my family to tell them not to worry, I worry!"

"I know it's hard Chi Wei, but you can't go on thinking so negatively and tempting the gods of misfortune. You will drive yourself crazy. And you will surely make me a nervous wreck if I have to hear your bloodcurdling screams every other night!"

Ning Yang, thought Chi Wei, has been a good friend ever since we met on the boat coming over. Digging in the mines side by side during the day and sharing a tent at night, we have spent many hours talking about life back home and life in Gam Saan. But despite his words, mulled Chi Wei, I am still uneasy about how we Chinese are treated in this foreign place.

"I am sure that some of the stories we hear may have some truth to them. But that's why we stick together in big groups," continued Ning Yang. "Even though we can only keep half of the gold we mine while the rest goes to the mining company, there is safety in numbers. And there are what, thirty or forty of us together in this camp? As wild as some of the white miners can be, even in their most drunken state, I don't think they would be so stupid as to attack all of us at one time," assured Ning Yang.

"Why do you think the white men treat us so unkindly, as if we are below them? We are not allowed to claim any rights. We are only permitted to work the mines they have left behind. They don't treat us as equals or respect us as men. I often feel like they treat their mules and dogs better than us," commented Chi Wei.

"Yeah, and although those white devils never seem to bathe like we do every night, and grow their hair all over their faces and bodies, we are the ones treated like animals," added Ning Yang wryly, with a mischievous twinkle in his eyes.

"This is the way I see it," continued Ning Yang philosophically. "We are a different breed of men because we are sons of Han. But yes, in the end, whether from China or across the other oceans, we are all still men. Unfortunately, it is human nature to be suspicious of those who are different.

Chinese people are just as guilty as others. The fact that all of us are here for the same reason makes us competitors. And though there is probably enough gold for everyone, we are all greedy. We don't want others, especially not our 'own kind,' to get what we think is rightfully ours.

"Obviously we look different. We have black hair, and they have hair of gold or flaming fire. We are clean-shaven with long hair, neatly tied and braided in the back, while they have tangled short and sometimes curly hair, with more hair growing under their nose and mouth." He then pulled the end of his queue under his nose, miming the bushy moustaches of the white miners. Chi Wei couldn't help but crack a smile.

Chi Wei watched Ning Yang waving his arms, bowing, and making gestures characteristic of both Chinese and white miners. "Sometimes, I think you should become a professional storyteller, or an actor with the Chinese Opera," he told his friend. Ning Yang just waved away Chi Wei's comments and continued.

"We do almost everything differently because of our Confucian upbringing. We have been taught to have a high regard for order and restraint. The pale-skinned miners appear to be, especially after the consumption of their whiskey, wild and untamed. Yet, they consider us heathens because we don't believe in their gods. We both find each other's language strange and unnerving, with sounds unfamiliar to our ears. Yet, this I know to be a fact: we definitely eat better. Hot steamed rice is far superior to dry bread!"

"Ning Yang, you are always the clown, but there is much truth in what you say. Do you think that men will ever change? Do you think we will ever be welcomed here?" Chi Wei asked pensively.

"You have to remember, too, Chi Wei, that not all of them are like that. Some of them are just as peaceful and fair as we are and are worthy of our respect. But quite frankly, Chi Wei, I don't think about it that much. I just try and keep out of their way, mind my own business, and save my money so I can get back home with all my riches. I am just here for a short time."

"Do you think that's what makes the white miners even more angry with us -- because we're taking the gold from this country and returning to our own?" asked Chi Wei."

"No, I think they would be more unhappy if we planned to stay. But no Han son in his right mind would want to stay here among the foreign devils!" exclaimed Ning Yang.

"Well, I don't know about that, but I'm with you in that I will only stay as long as it takes to make my fortune. I was talking to Yin Jun, our cook, however, and he is actually considering making a life here! His parents died last spring; they were victims of the village feuds. So, he says there's nothing to return to but their graves. He has no wife or children back home, so he is on his own. He says he's getting used to the life here, and he feels a sense of freedom here that he never felt before in China."

"Ah, Yin Jun, he is an excellent cook. I bet you he could make a life for himself here cooking for other people. If he wasn't our cook, I'd be willing to pay for his food," agreed Ning Yang. "In fact, after I strike it rich, I would be willing to take Yin Jun back with me to be my own personal cook, because as a prosperous gentleman, I could afford him. He would relieve my wife of all her duties in the kitchen. And Chi Wei, I miss my wife, but believe me, I can certainly do without her cooking!"

"I don't think Yin Jun would be interested in working for you, Ning Yang, no matter how rich you become. Sometimes, he tells me that he dreams of moving on, and maybe opening a restaurant in one of the larger towns near the harbors. He says that you would be surprised how many of the white miners have ventured out and taken a liking to Chinese cooking, though they don't readily admit it. Yin Jun said they are fascinated with the variety of ways the Chinese people have managed to cook our food, like stir-frying, steaming, and sautéing," added Chi Wei.

"Did I not tell you before that we eat better than the barbarians? But enough of this talk about food. You are making my mouth water and I am too sleepy to eat. Let us talk more tomorrow. If we do not try to rest, we will be useless when the sun rises," yawned Ning Yang. "Try dreaming about feasting on Yin Jun's cooking this time, Chi Wei, so you'll wake up with a full belly instead of a cold sweat," mumbled Ning Yang as he fell fast asleep.

"Thank you my dear friend," Chi Wei whispered in the darkness. It was comforting for him to hear Ning Yang's steady snoring as he thought about the camaraderie that had developed between the two of them. Ning Yang's words of encouragement and wit always helped alleviate his pangs of loneliness. Without a wife and family, the next best thing was to have a friend like Ning Yang by your side.

chapter 7

"Grammy, it sounds like this Chi Wei guy had more problems than just being called bad names," I said. "Do you think that things were that bad -- that Chinese miners were chased and beaten?"

"I'm afraid so, Christie. You have to remember that everyone was competing for gold at that time. Gold and greed, along with prejudice, can do funny things to people. Even though there was so much gold to be discovered, some white miners resented any success the Chinese miners had."

"That letter sounded sad, like he was really homesick," said Michael.

"It wasn't easy being so far from home, but at least he had some companionship, which helped him carry on. The fact that the Chinese miners banded together really helped them all to survive. It sounds like they found ways to relax, talk, and entertain themselves through music and games."

"Yeah, I liked the part about playing checkers and chess. I didn't know that Chinese knew how to play those games back them," said Michael, an avid chess player himself. "What does the next one say, Grammy?"

Dear Papa and Mama,

I have been here for over a year and the work is hard. We do not hear about home very often. I hope my meager savings of $25 will help you buy food for Chung An and Ying Ying as well as yourselves. I miss you all very much.

I am thinking that I will stop mining and get a job with one of the well-to-do white men, living in his house doing chores. There is a family in town looking for a Chinese man to do their cooking, laundry, and cleaning. I know it sounds like women's work, but it pays well and there is no disgrace in it. It pays about $5 a week which is not bad, and certainly a lot more than I could make in China.

Mining is too hard for me. My arms, legs, and back ache every night from using the heavy pickax to dig into the mine walls. Panning for gold in the icy streams is not any easier and takes a lot of patience. I have found that men like me can still make a good amount of money by seeking out other opportunities. The couple that is will-

ing to hire me seem to be very nice. The husband is a doctor, and the wife lived in China at one time because her parents were Christian missionaries there. She speaks Cantonese. You would be amazed at how well she speaks our tongue!

Don't worry, Mama, I don't plan on converting to their religion. They have earned a very good reputation among the Chinese because they have been very kind and helpful to those who have problems or who cannot communicate with the authorities here. Best of all, I have heard that they are willing to teach their workers how to speak English. I think this is the key to success here for I have seen how those who know the language become very successful in business ventures.

I know that this is a change from what you expected of me, but I am finding that there are many ways to find gold here.

I will write you again soon.

With much respect,
Chiu Sang

"How did you and Grandpa learn to speak

English, Grammy?" I asked.

"Well, Grandpa was born here so he learned it in school. He, of course, spoke Cantonese at home. When he came to China to marry me and bring me with him back to California, I knew no English at all. I know all too well what it must have been like for those miners to come here and not be able to understand the language. At first I felt very lost and confused. I tried to communicate with hand motions, but after awhile it became very frustrating. Sometimes, I felt stupid because I could not communicate. You really have to be determined and set your mind on learning because English is so very different than Chinese. In English, you have a 26-letter alphabet, with each letter representing a sound, while the Chinese have thousands of symbols that are actual words."

"So did someone teach you or did you take classes, because your English is really good."

"Well, basically, I taught myself with the help of a Chinese-English dictionary that I took everywhere. It was very hard for me because I was accustomed to using one Chinese character per word; and one slight change in sound could change the entire meaning of a word from something like 'mother' to 'horse.' In English, you have to put together a group of sounds to make up just one word. A friend would come over and help me pronounce the words. I can still remember her slowly and patiently going over each vowel and consonant with me.

chapter 8

"Chiu Sang, this is the letter "O." Listen carefully now and watch my mouth make an "O." Let's see if you can make the same sound," instructed Mrs. Sarah.

Taking a deep breath, Chiu Sang slowly made a circle with his lips and repeated the sound "O" to Mrs. Sarah.

Mrs. Sarah smiled and said "Good. Now, let me give you some words to practice and we'll finish our lesson for today. It's hard to believe that we've been doing this for just three months. You really are catching on quickly. I am very proud of your progress. We'll continue tomorrow," said Mrs. Sarah as she got up to leave the room

Sitting alone, Chiu Sang continued to carefully round his lips to pronounce the words in front of him: 'old,' 'over,' 'open.' He pondered how his world had completely changed in just three months. He recalled his first meeting with Dr. John

Stanley, Mrs. Sarah's husband. He was the only white doctor in town who would go to the mines to help the Chinese miners when they became ill or injured. Chiu Sang had broken his arm and Dr. John had come to tend to it. He had heard stories about Dr. John and his wife. Mrs. Sarah was a missionary's daughter who spoke flawless Cantonese, which almost always took the Chinese by surprise when they met her. After finally meeting the doctor and his wife, Chiu Sang could see why they were highly regarded and well-respected. They were kind and compassionate, and maybe more importantly, they treated the Chinese as fellow human beings. Their reputation allowed them to become trusted liaisons between two contrasting worlds.

Initially, when Dr. John offered to hire Chiu Sang to do chores in his home, Chiu Sang thought that he would disgrace his family by giving up gold mining to go into household service. But after weighing his options, he decided that this opportunity might be best for him, and in the long run, his family back home. He had been on Gold Mountain for two years, having come over when he was 15. His father had just lost his job as a dock worker on the harbor when the British took over the port. Being an ambitious young man, Chiu Sang had convinced his parents that there were many more opportunities across the ocean. At first his father was reluctant because he doubted that Chiu Sang, with his slight build, had the strength and stamina it would take to survive. Now, as Chiu Sang looked back on this, he conceded that his father was right, as he remembered how physically taxing mining had been for him. But now things were different.

The English lessons came surprisingly easy for him, and Mrs. Sarah was always saying that he was a quick learner. Chiu Sang was also starting to realize just how many opportunities could open up if he were able to master this new language.

Though he worked from sun up to sundown doing household chores, Chiu Sang genuinely enjoyed working for the Stanley family. He especially liked being around the children because they reminded him of his own younger brother and sister back home. Though they didn't speak the same language, they were still able to find ways to communicate. The children would often point to different items in the room and tell him how to say the words. Chiu Sang smiled to himself as he remembered their laughter at some of his pronunciations. But like their mother, they were patient and helpful until he finally got it right. I know I have a long way to go, but I am pleased with the progress I'm making, reflected Chiu Sang.

He enjoyed making the two Stanley children smile and laugh. One of their favorite things was watching him iron their father's dress shirts. He knew that he could always make them roar with laughter when he filled his mouth with water until his cheeks puffed out and then deflated them as he sprayed a mist over the shirts. In those moments, he could almost hear the happy sounds of his siblings far across the ocean.

No, thought Chiu Sang to himself, he certainly didn't miss life in the mining camps. He felt very fortunate to be with this family. The fact that Mrs. Sarah could talk to him in Chinese alleviated some of his feelings of isolation, though he still missed his family and his Chinese friends in the camps. But so far, he hadn't regretted the decision to become a paid servant and part of the Stanley household. His life was certainly taking an unexpected direction.

The house in which he now lived had many rooms and was quite a contrast to a typical Chinese house. The two Stanley children each had their own bedroom, which was unheard of in China, as most families slept all together. There was even a room just for Dr. John's books where Chiu Sang's English lessons took place which they called the 'library.' He slept in a relatively small room next to the kitchen, which was more than enough room for him. And it was certainly more pleasant than sleeping in a tent out in the open. He still, however, had not gotten used to the soft mattress and feathery pillow, since he was much more accustomed to putting his head on the curved wooden pillow that he had brought from China.

The walls of the house were decorated with painted flower designs, and the windows were covered with delicate lace. There were many paintings and family photographs that hung on the walls. It was a huge contrast to the simple and stark surroundings that Chiu Sang had known most of his life.

There were always chores to be done through-out this large house. He got up with the sun and worked through the early evening. Though the hours were long, it was not as physically draining as mining for gold. Now having some security from a steady wage, Chiu Sang faithfully saved most of his weekly paycheck and sent it home to his parents. His English lessons with Mrs. Sarah and their trips into town were his highlights.

As a way to boost his vocabulary, Mrs. Sarah had started taking him to the general store in town so that he could help carry back groceries and sup-plies. She would use the time to teach him words and customs. Although he did not yet know the right words, he felt the townspeople were polite to him only because Mrs. Sarah had taken him under her wing. He knew that many of them regarded him as an oddity, but as time went on, others went out of their way to be helpful and befriend him.

It was clear to Chiu Sang that Dr. John and Mrs. Sarah were deeply religious people. They prayed at mealtime, though he didn't know to whom they were praying since he never noticed any family altars in the dining room or anywhere else in the house. He also noted that on the day of the week called 'Sunday,' the entire family would dress in their finest clothes and go to their house of worship.

One Sunday they invited him to go with them. Although he knew that should his mother ever find out she would be quite angry, Chiu Sang figured that one visit would not hurt. His parents, like most traditional Chinese families, embraced all religions and followed Confucian, Buddhist, and Taoist rituals in their home. He had visited the local Chinese temple when he'd arrived and burned incense to honor his ancestors and to thank the gods for a safe journey. This temple was just a simple room that had been faithfully modeled after the temples back home -- complete with the decorative altars painted bright red and gold, colorful banners on long wooden sticks, and porcelain figurines representing the various Chinese deities.

When the Stanleys and Chiu Sang arrived at the Christian church, Chiu Sang was struck by the austerity of the simple white wooden structure with a cross hanging above the doorway. It was a marked contrast to the tall, red-painted columns, curved, tiled roofs, and elaborate carvings that were characteristic of Chinese temples. The church interior was just as plain. There were no carvings, statues, or any religious symbols, with the exception of a small white wooden cross placed on a table in the front of the room. The smell of burning incense, always present in Chinese temples, was noticeably absent.

Toward the front of the room sat a musical instrument that he had never seen before; they called it a 'piano.' A man sat down on a bench and played this piano with his fingers. Wonderful sounds filled the room. Then everyone stood up and sang songs together. This was certainly different from the simple chanting of Buddhist priests.

The people gathered at the church that morning appeared very friendly as they smiled and shook his hands, a custom he was still getting used to, as he instinctively bowed to each person. Mrs. Sarah also introduced him to three other Chinese men about his age. Apparently, these were the men that Mrs. Sarah also gave English lessons to during the week. Chiu Sang wondered if these men were there out of obligation to Mrs. Sarah and were listening attentively out of politeness, as was he.

Mrs. Sarah motioned him to sit down. He saw that everyone else was seated, too. A man in a dark suit stood up at the front of the church and read from a large black book. Chiu Sang noticed that Mrs. Sarah and the three Chinese men had similar books. After everything was finished, the four of them talked back and forth in English and Chinese but most of the time Chiu Sang felt quite lost. He surmised that this book must have great significance and importance to this religion.

All in all the experience at the Christian church was quite pleasant. He felt fairly sure that his mother would not have to worry about him turning away from the Chinese gods. Though he found himself willing to adapt to many of the Western ways, the gap that separated Eastern and Western religious ideas was seemingly far too wide to overcome. The practice of praying to just one invisible deity or worshipping the cross as a symbol of death was incomprehensible to him. He wondered how on earth could only one god be able to help all men. The Chinese had many different gods for every place and occasion. There was a god of mercy, one for good fortune, and one for long life, as well as gods that controlled the growth of crops and the rain, among other things.

He was, however, intrigued by the leather book with gold pages, and was fascinated with the discussion he overheard between Mrs. Sarah and the three other Chinese gentlemen. Sensing his interest, the three of them invited him to tea the following week. He gladly accepted, always willing to get together with fellow countrymen.

It was a common practice for the Chinese sojourners to gather at the "Little China" part of town. Chiu Sang looked forward to his free afternoons when he could sip tea with his companions, exchange thoughts and stories, and hear about news from back home. Sometimes his friends would tease him about becoming too much like the pale barbarians and maybe even 'Christianized' by the female missionary. But others encouraged him to keep up his English lessons. They saw that he was a quick learner and had a sharp mind that would benefit him in whatever he chose to pursue. Perhaps they knew, deep down, that he would not always be a houseboy. They knew as well as he, that this was just a stepping-stone in his journey up the Gold Mountain.

chapter 9

"Grammy, you sure did a good job of teaching yourself how to speak English, because you talk good now," said Michael with obvious pride.

"That's 'speak well,' Michael, not 'talk good'," I countered, rolling my eyes.

"Now, you two, I think I make that same mistake all the time. But I really did have to work hard to learn a new language, and even to this day, I have trouble with certain words," Grammy admitted.

"Like the word 'syrup' huh, Grammy?" I said with a smile. "It is always funny when you ask for the 'shirrup' at breakfast."

"Yes, Christie," laughed Grammy, "for some reason my tongue has a hard time with that word."

"Christie, Michael!" yelled Grandpa from outside, "Auntie Mei is here!"

We jumped up leaving the letters behind and ran outside. Grandpa's Auntie Mei is real old. I don't think she even knows how old she really is. Mom thinks she's probably around 95 years old, but as Mom puts it, "She's sharp as a tack."

Grandpa helps her out of the car, and, of course, she's pushing his hand away. She is always trying to show us that she can still do things on her own.

"Hi, my favorite little ones," she says, as she squeezes our cheeks until we squirm away. I turn to Michael and whisper, "For a frail old woman, she sure has some powerful pinchers!"

Auntie Mei looks like your typical old Chinese lady with her hair tightly combed back into a neat bun that stays in place with a tortoise shell barrette. She wears tiny gold-rimmed glasses and jade-button earrings. When she smiles, you can see a line of gold-filled teeth. Though she was born and raised in this country, she still prefers to wear the blue Chinese-styled top with a high collar and loose-fitting pants.

Even though her appearance is fairly typical, she's far from your run-of-the-mill, only-speaks-Chinese-to-you, great-grand-aunt type. She's strong as an ox, real funny, and what a memory! Every time we visit Grandpa and Grammy, we spend a little time with her. She always has tons of stories to tell us about the old days.

"Look at the two of you! You both are getting so tall! I think you are almost taller than me!" exclaims Auntie Mei, as she looks us over.

I think she must be all of 4'7", so even Michael is about her height.

"Christie, you are too skinny. You need to fatten up. But you, Michael, I can tell you've been eating well," teases Auntie Mei, patting his round stomach. "It's good to have Grandma's cooking, yes?"

"Oh, Auntie Mei, you were right!" I can hardly wait to tell her. "There really is a hidden room in this old house, just like you said. It's behind the wall of the big closet. We found some old letters from the 1850s there, and Grammy's been reading them to us. I'll go get them to show you! Then it suddenly occurred to me, "Auntie Mei, do you think these letters were never sent because the storekeeper was killed?"

Auntie Mei looked at me with amazement. "I guess that would make the most sense. You really found the room? I can't believe it! All these years I've been telling the same old story, but I never believed a word of it . . . it was just a good story, yes?"

"Let me show it to you, Auntie Mei!" insists Michael.

"In a minute, Michael. But you say that you found letters, Christie?"

"Yes, five of them. We haven't read this last one yet. Do you want to read it for us, Auntie Mei?"

"Oh, Christie, Auntie Mei would like to, but her eyes can't see such small writing. Let's have your Grammy read it, but I am very interested in hearing what it says."

Grammy finishes pouring tea for Auntie Mei. "Okay, let's see what's in this last letter!" she says as she takes a seat beside me on the sofa.

Dear Auntie,

I know my mama is still angry with me for coming to Gam Saan with my husband. Maybe someday she will understand that I had to come to be with Pu Yan . . .

"Pu Yan, why does that name ring a bell?" interrupted Auntie Mei. "Oh, I'm sorry, keep reading. It'll come to me." I looked up at Auntie Mei and I could tell that she was really thinking hard about something because she had a puzzled look on her face. Grammy continued reading the letter.

Maybe someday she will understand that I had to come to be with Pu Yan, and that this was an opportunity that I could not pass up. Tell her that she doesn't need to worry about what other people are saying about me, a woman, going to a foreign land.

We are visiting Mr. Lee, a friend of Pu Yan's father, and he is writing this letter for me. In a few days we will leave by boat for a smaller town called Monterey, just south of San Francisco.

We will be helping Fay Hung, Pu Yan's cousin, with his store in Monterey. There are more and more Chinese settling in this area, and the demand for things from the homeland is very high. The men want to wear the more comfortable cotton pants and jackets made in China. They also want the large straw hats that we use in the fields for protection from the sun when they are working outside the mines. I think that our business venture will be successful someday.

Monterey is a seaport town. Some of the Chinese men have taken up fishing for mackerel, shrimp and abalone because there is so much to be caught here. Cousin Fay Hung says they want us to send their dried shrimp back to China and sell them there. I told him that it is a very good idea.

There are very few women. The white women who are here have been very friendly to me. I think that they think I am very strange and unusual, but I think the same of them! Yet, there is a common bond because we are women. There are not very many Chinese women here, so I appreciate how these women have reached out to me. The only way that we can communicate is with our hands. Pu Yan says that if we stay here for any length of time that we should try and learn English. I don't know if I can learn it, but I would like to, as it seems impossible to live here without knowing the language, as strange as it is to our ears.

It is difficult not to get caught up in the excitement of Gam Saan, where everyone dreams of being the next poor man to become rich overnight. In truth, living, working and surviving here is hard work. Sometimes I wish for the servants we had back home. And yet, in spite of that, being here in this new country gives me a sense of freedom I have never felt before. I am realizing that the world is much bigger than just China, and Gam Saan has more to offer than just gold. There are so many things to see and experience. Here we can carve out our *own future and destiny, and that is exciting!*

Mama probably doesn't want to hear such things coming from me, but back in China I felt like a caged bird. Here in Gam Saan, I can fly freely.

I shall write again soon.

Affectionately yours,
Shau Ching

chapter 10

Once Grammy finished reading the letter and saying the writer's name, Auntie Mei's eyes lit up and got really big as she almost shouted out loud, "Pu Yan! Shau Ching! They were married. I knew a Shau Ching, a Lee Shau Ching, when I was a little girl!"

"Of course, she was an old woman then like I am today, and I called her 'Auntie Ching,' but this sounds like the very same woman. The Shau Ching I knew was a merchant's wife, and one of the first respectable women to come over to these parts. Pu Yan worked in his cousin's store, not this one here, another one. After awhile they branched out toward Monterey. Even after her husband died, Auntie Ching kept up the business and proved to be quite a remarkable businesswoman herself," explained Auntie Mei.

I didn't know about anyone else in the room, but I was totally amazed at the thought that Auntie Mei actually may have known one of these letter writers!

Auntie Mei continued by telling us that as a young child, she used to sit on Auntie Ching's lap and listen to her tell stories, kind of like how Michael and I used to sit on Auntie Mei's lap when we were a lot smaller. She said that Shau Ching was not related by blood, but all the children called her "Auntie Ching" as a sign of affection because she was so well-liked by everyone.

Auntie Mei remembered Auntie Ching telling her about how she and her husband, Pu Yan, had only been married for a few months when his cousin wrote from the Gold Mountain and asked him to join him in a business venture. Auntie Mei must have heard this story a dozen times or more, because as she started telling it to us, it was as if she was reciting it from recent memory.

"Pu Yan had always been an adventurous type, and the lure of distant lands was very tempting to him. Shau Ching, known by all for her independent spirit, convinced him to take her along. In those days, it was very uncommon for women to immigrate to Gam Saan because it went against the Chinese custom of wives staying with the family.

"And most of the women who did land on

these shores didn't come here by choice. It was not uncommon for desperate and starving families to sell their daughters. These women, actually still young girls, were then sold into slavery when they arrived here."

"What, Auntie Mei?" I interrupted her in disbelief. "Did that really happen?"

She assured me that she was not making it up and that life back then was extremely different than it is now. She added that girls were not as valued as boys in Chinese society, and this was especially true in poor families.

"But back to Shau Ching," continues Auntie Mei, "she had no such worries. She grew up sheltered and pampered, like a little princess used to getting her way. Her mother was so embarrassed with her total disregard for Confucian ideas and felt so disgraced by her unruly behavior, that she refused to speak to her again. But Shau Ching had to get her stubbornness from somewhere, right? Well, once she decided that she wanted to go with Pu Yan, no one could stop her."

chapter 11

"Fay Hung, is this your cousin's wife?" Mrs. Thompson asked, as she entered the store. "I've been meaning to stop by and meet her. I never see her walking about in town, so I thought I should come by the store."

"I glad you come," Fay Hung responded in his best English. Mrs. Thompson, one of the friendlier women in these parts, often frequented Fay Hung's store. He realized that she did not understand that he and Pu Yan had to be extremely protective of Shau Ching, making sure she was under their watchful eyes at all times. They did not allow her to go out in public, for fear that she would be attacked, or even kidnapped, by unruly white miners. He was, however, glad that Mrs. Thompson came to welcome his cousin's wife, as she would probably benefit from the companionship of another woman, since women, and especially Chinese women, were rare sights.

"Well, I just made some muffins and thought you would enjoy them," Mrs. Thompson told them.

Fay Hung motioned to Shau Ching to come over to Mrs. Thompson so he could introduce them. As Shau Ching bowed, the sweet aroma of cinnamon tickled her nose. Mrs. Thompson then unwrapped the napkin and placed one in Shau Ching's hand. "Go ahead and try it, Shau Ching," she encouraged.

Shau Ching didn't quite know what to make of this small, round-shaped cake that was warming the palm of her hand. But she could no longer politely resist the tempting smell, so she hesitantly took a bite. It was delicious, and she broke into a big smile. Mrs. Thompson let out a hearty laugh. "I think she likes it, Fay Hung, and I think I have made a new friend."

This was the first of Shau Ching's many encounters with Mrs. Thompson who had taken a special liking to her. Mrs. Thompson had never had any children of her own, so she took young Shau Ching under her wing and treated her as a daughter. Not only did Mrs. Thompson teach her English, but also how to bake muffins and cookies. Shau Ching, in turn, introduced Mrs. Thompson to some of the more exotic Chinese delicacies that arrived in the store and how to embroider delicate designs on fine silk. Shau Ching was learning, day by day, the American ways from Mrs. Thompson. Although she missed home, she reveled in her newfound freedom, no longer bound by the strict rules of Chinese customs.

Shau Ching suspected Fay Hung regretted that Pu Yan's decision to bring his young wife with him, and wanted very much to prove to them both that it wasn't a mistake. One day, after noticing the large piles of bills, orders, and receipts on top of the counter, she offered to put the papers in order.

"I don't know how Fay Hung can be such a successful businessman when he is so messy and disorganized," muttered Shau Ching to herself as she began sorting through the various pieces of paper, separating them into individual piles. Within a few hours, Fay Hung couldn't believe his eyes as he surveyed the uncluttered countertop. All his papers were divided by account -- who owed and who paid -- and filed neatly into boxes.

"Shau Ching, you have done an excellent job here. Pu Yan has not only chosen a beautiful wife, but a capable one as well."

From that point on, Fay Hung put Shau Ching in charge of keeping track of inventory and sales. Both Fay Hung and Pu Yan quickly recognized Shau Ching's special talents and keen mind, but especially, her gift for numbers. Contrary to the traditional Chinese way of thinking which limited a woman's input in affairs "reserved for men," the three of them shared and developed ideas to expand their business.

Fay Hung was acquainted with many of the Chinese sojourners who decided to seek their fortune in the ocean rather than in the mountains. The Chinese fishermen used a method from the old country of preserving the fish they caught by covering them with plenty of salt and spreading them out to dry under the sun. The salted fish, or shrimp, became a staple for the miners because it was lightweight to carry, and when cooked, turned steamed rice and vegetables into delicious meals.

The Monterey region was a fisherman's paradise. There was just about every imaginable fish -- as well as oysters, shrimp, and sea cucumbers. Pu Yan and Shau Ching persuaded Fay Hung to start shipping the abundance of salted shrimp back to China. This became such a profitable endeavor that Pu Yan and Shau Ching expanded the exporting operations to include dried and salted squid, herring, clams, and seaweed. Such an opportunity would never have materialized in China, but this was the land of the Gold Mountain.

chapter 12

"So did Shau Ching's mother ever forgive her, Auntie Mei?" I asked curiously.

"Sad to say, Christie, but she never did. I still remember very clearly that even as an old woman, tears would come to Auntie Ching's eyes when she spoke about the mother who was lost to her. She did mention an American woman who was very nice and was almost like a mother to her. But I think this auntie to whom she was writing must have been her only link to her family back in China.

"That's so sad. Do you remember anything else about her?" I asked, hoping that Auntie Mei could tell me more about the woman behind this letter.

"When Shau Ching and her husband started working in Fay Hung's store, the business was just for selling basic supplies for the Chinese sojourners. Soon though, business expanded with the demand for all kinds of different foods and merchandise for not just locals, but miners and eventually, even abroad. Chinese people have always enjoyed good seafood and had invented all kinds of ways to catch, treat, and cook it like no one else. So Fay Hung, Pu Yan, and Shau Ching, what do you call it, 'capitalized' on the great demand in China for the dried and salted fish and shrimp provided by the Chinese fishermen of Monterey. So what was once a small family business turned into a very successful exporting operation."

"Auntie Mei, is that salted fish the same as the one Grandpa likes so much? You know, the really stinky kind you find in Chinese grocery stores," Michael asked, as he pinched his nose imagining the smell.

"Yes, Michael, they are similar," answered Auntie Mei, as Michael and I looked at each other and in unison said, "Yuck!"

Auntie Mei continued her story. "Auntie Ching told us that a few Chinese fisherman had discovered a place where there was an unbelievable amount of abalone. You see, Californians, at that time, did not even eat abalone. But dried abalone had been a favorite Chinese delicacy for many years. So within months the entire area was swarming with Chinese abalone seekers.

"Even the abalone shells didn't go to waste. Tons of them were sent to China to make those beautiful pearl inlaid designs you see on Chinese cabinets, tables, and jewelry. You can be sure that these shells certainly made a pretty penny for those fishermen," Auntie Mei exclaimed.

"Auntie Ching," she continued, "said it was like another kind of gold rush, and that their business, though successful through the years, never experienced anything like the . . . what shall I call it . . . 'Abalone Boom.' "

"You're kidding us now, Auntie Mei! An 'Abalone Boom'?" laughs Michael. "Or do you really mean 'Baloney Boom'?" he said, laughing harder at his own joke.

"Why do you children always think I make these things up?" smiles Auntie Mei. "Of course I didn't make this up! Everything I've been telling you is what I remember my Auntie Ching telling me. She was the very best storyteller, and I always believed everything she told me."

I could tell by looking at Auntie Mei's eyes that she was remembering herself way back then, sitting on her Auntie Ching's lap. I, too, couldn't help but think about what an incredible morning we had had. The hidden room had been uncovered and inside were these wonderful letters. What a discovery we had made! As Grammy had read each one, it was as if she were uncovering secret treasures one after the other. And then, to have our very own Auntie Mei actually know one of the writers made me realize how exciting history can be.

I shivered. Each letter had a voice that had spoken directly to me, telling us of hopes, feelings, fears, and dreams. With just a few words, their world came alive to me, more than 150 years later. It was as if we had been transported to another time and place. It was hard not to wonder what had happened to these letter writers and all the rest of the Chinese immigrants. I could only guess that some found their gold, while others did not. Many probably went back to China as they had always hoped to do. Others probably stayed, making the Gold Mountain their home and discovering other ways of making their fortune. Either way, I felt good getting to know them, even slightly, all these years later.

While we may never find the gold Grandpa said is under the store, each one of these letters in my hands is like a gold nugget. Yes, today we have definitely struck our own gold!

Afterword
by Yvonne M. Lau

While America is known as a country of immigrants, experiencing at the start of this new millennium the highest influx of new arrivals, the history of some ethnic groups overshadows others. As students in primary and secondary school systems or even in higher education, we are given disproportionate access to an Eurocentric curriculum. Most U.S. social studies and history classes focus on immigration by targeting the flood of southern and eastern Europeans at the dawn of the 20th century, and adopting European-based models of immigration and acculturation. Despite major demographic shifts in immigration patterns in the post-'65 era, reflecting major waves of immigrants from Asia, Latin America, and the Caribbean to the U.S., both popular culture and academic literature continue to marginalize those groups that have historically been underrepresented.

Searching for other immigrant stories involving non-European heroes and heroines, requires a bit of detective work and extra effort, as shown by Christie, our young heroine. To overcome the cultural biases prevalent in public and private school curricula, we need to uncover more "secret rooms" revealing stories of the often nameless "others" who built and shaped America. Provocative in many ways, this story is groundbreaking in how it provides young readers with an accurate depiction of one invisible group, Chinese American pioneers.

In the 19th Century, Chinese immigration to America was fueled by economic reasons, stemming from Southern China and the American West. Although a limited number of Chinese lived in the U.S. before the discovery of gold in 1848 – mainly merchants and sailors – large waves began in 1852 when over 50,000 came over. While the "pull" factors included fortune-seeking and basic needs to make a living and fill one's "ricebowl," the "push" factors included fleeing from political and economic chaos in China.

To understand the specifics underlying these push factors, we need to zoom in on the primary sending province, Guangdong (Kwangtung), which accounted for the vast majority of Chinese immigrants to California. Canton, the premier port city in Guangdong province, dominated in foreign trade, as early as the 7th century. Its importance diminished in the 13th century yet flourished as a pivotal trade city again throughout the 18th until mid-19th centuries.

In the Opium Wars with China, where the victors, Great Britain and other Western powers, forced the opening of China to trade and infusion of Christianity, key cities like Canton lost power and status. Cantonese of all backgrounds and occupations lost their livelihoods. Dockworkers, cottage industry workers, peasants, and farmers were all negatively affected as high taxes were imposed to help pay the indemnity mandated by the Treaty of Nanjing. The flood of opium by British importers to reverse the balance of trade with China, also took a heavy toll on the residents as addiction rose dramatically.

The increasing presence of Westerners and foreign ships brought more opportunities for labor recruiters to entice young peasants abroad, bypassing the government law prohibiting emigration. Civil unrest, including the Taiping Rebellion, prevailed through much of Southern China, from 1850-64, causing regional famines and family hardships in the area. Just as Wong Meng laments about not having much of a choice, emigration was not merely a path to gold and fortune, but a necessity for survival.

When the first major wave of Chinese arrived in the U.S. in the 1850's, the American West was a frontier. With a limited pool of workers in California, especially European Americans, the earliest Chinese pioneers were able to find jobs in a variety of fields including work as miners, railroad workers, domestics, and farmers. Yet as increasing numbers of European Americans established communities on the West Coast by the 1870's, they wanted to monopolize the more lucrative fields. Particularly after the completion of the first transcontinental railroad in 1869 and the closing of most mines, Chinese encountered more resistance and restrictions, and were relegated to menial jobs in low-wage industries and service niches.

As the story mentions, special taxes and

legislation aimed at the Chinese were common-place, ranging from local ordinances to later, national policies. Discriminatory legislation towards "non-whites" resulted in excluding Chinese and other Asians from high-paying jobs including unionized jobs. Occupation-specific restrictions included not only the story's special gold tax for Chinese miners (1850), but examples like the San Francisco Laundry Ordinance (1880) and Sidewalk Ordinance (1870). The latter prohibited the Chinese pole method of selling vegetables and carrying laundry in San Francisco. Chinese traditionally would carry heavy items on a pole, balanced on their shoulders. The ordinance was targeted at Chinese since others used carts to sell their goods.

Other laws directed at Chinese included the Cubic Air (1871) and Queue Ordinances (1873). The former law regulated that each adult have at least 500 cubic feet of living space in San Francisco. Aimed against the Chinese who were restricted to crowded living conditions in the ethnic ghettoes, the law was fueled by anti-Chinese sentiments. The Queue ordinance similarly discriminated against Chinese by outlawing queues or the long braids worn by Chinese men. During the Manchu dynasty, Chinese men were forced to wear these long braids; removal or cutting of the braids was a serious breach of Chinese law, denying them any hope of returning to China. With the Anti-Queue law, Chinese men were attacked often by groups of thugs who would wear queues as trophies.

Growing anti-Chinese resentment and economic competition with Whites culminated in several anti-Chinese campaigns primarily on the West Coast. Laws excluded Chinese from jobs in federal, state, county, or city governments. In time, the Chinese were eventually barred from the fishing industry in California.

For the very few numbers of Chinese children in this early period, there were laws prohibiting their education in public schools in San Francisco, restricting them to a separate school as early as 1859; it later closed due to low enrollments. Twenty-five years later, the parents of Mamie Tape challenged the San Francisco School Board's denial of their daughter's right to a public education. Due to their efforts, an "Oriental School" was established in 1885. Segregated schools predominated not only in San Francisco, but in other delta communities of California until the 1930s.

Chinese were denied access to basic civil rights because of their legal status as "aliens." Deemed "ineligible" for citizenship, they were barred from testifying in courts against white defendants, and prohibited from owning or leasing land for more than three years. They were allowed to buy property only in San Francisco Chinatown. Chinese and other Asian immigrants were also disproportionately impacted by anti-miscegenation laws prohibiting marriage between races. The California legislature restricted marriages between a white person and a "negro, mulatto or Mongolian" (1880).

These anti-miscegenation laws, coupled with laws restricting the entry of Chinese women, served to confine many Chinese men to the "bachelor societies" dominating the Chinatown ghettoes. The Page Law (1875) was passed by Congress to prevent Chinese women from entering, drastically curtailing the numbers of women. For those Chinese men who gave up their "sojourner's dream" of returning to their homeland, they faced the harsh realities of living permanently in America without prospects of forming nuclear families. By the close of the 19th century, the male-female ratio for Chinese was 26:1; about 100,000 Chinese men and 4,000 Chinese women were living in the U.S. in 1890. Consequently, the last letter-writer in the story, Shau Ching, represents a rare case in the 19th century saga of Chinese American pioneers. As a young wife determined to migrate with her husband, Shau Ching arrived in this earlier, less restrictive period of the 1850s. Her class position coming from a wealthy family with servants places her in an elite circle that few Chinese American women enjoyed. Non-traditional in rebelling against the wishes of her family and accompanying her husband to the U.S. at the beginning of their marriage and career, she aspires not only to serve her husband, but to carry out her business ambitions. She asserts herself and earns recognition as a good wife and saavy businesswoman.

The nadir of anti-Chinese legislation occurs in 1882 when Congress passed the Chinese Exclusion Act, the first public policy barring a specific ethnic and occupational group from entering the U.S. The law prohibits Chinese laborers from entering the country for ten years, exempting diplomats, teachers, students, visitors, and merchants. Later legislation reconfirmed Congressional sentiment to eliminate or severely curtail the presence of Chinese laborers. The Scott Act (1888) and the Geary Act (1892) prohibited the entry or reentry of Chinese laborers. The Chinese Exclusion Act was extended each decade until 1904 when it was indefinitely extended. Beyond the mainland, Chinese were also restricted from entering new territories like Hawaii, Puerto Rico, and the Philippines.

Although the experiences of Chinese immigrants can be linked to other immigrant groups, there are clear contrasts. As recent arrivals in a country, many immigrant groups are subjected to ridicule and prejudice. Immigrants often start at the lowest rungs, limited by unfamiliarity with the dominant language and culture. Yet the Chinese were also restricted legally from pursuing career or social goals – restricted by racialized laws legitimating discrimination.

While some Chinese valiantly tried to "fight

back" and protest again oppressive conditions – filing suits, staging boycotts, or organizing workers – they were "politically challenged" for they had no political power. Without the rights of citizenship, they were unable to vote or lobby effectively for themselves.

What's inspiring about the story's letter-writers and characters is how they each strategized and met their multitude of challenges with courage and tenacity. Overcoming personal fears and public abuses, they believed in their dreams and took many risks. Despite the often hostile climate in the 19th century American West facing Chinese, these characters tried to fight back. Sometimes their ideas and actions made life better not for themselves, but for the "extended" family of co-ethnics or other Chinese.

Though these characters are fictional, the author has taken great care to infuse her story with accurate details of this pioneer era. Depicting realistic Chinese American pioneers in the American West frontier, she has provided her characters with "chi" or living energy. Transformed from nameless "hordes" into heroes and heroines, the stories of

Wong Meng, Wing Wah, Chi Wei, Chiu Sang, and Shau Ching, enhance our understanding of Chinese Americans - an immigrant group that has continued to play significant roles in building and shaping America.

Yvonne M. Lau

Yvonne M. Lau is Director of Asian and Asian American Studies at Loyola University Chicago. She holds an undergraduate degree from Cornell University and has a Ph.D. in Sociology from Northwestern University. She has served on the Executive Board of the Association for Asian American Studies and as past president of the Asian American Institute. Currently, she serves on the Council Section on Asia and Asian America of the American Sociological Association. Professor Lau also serves on the Illinois State Board of Education's Bias Review Committee and on the Editorial Board of *The Chicago Reporter*.

Professor Lau's research interests include race, gender & class, immigrant & minority labor markets, minorities in secondary and higher education, and social policy. She has undertaken research on how race-based policies have shaped the experiences and status of Asian American students in higher education. Current research interests include conducting a comparative analysis of the educational experiences and outcomes of racial and linguistic minorities in a major urban public school system.

Acknowledgements

Polychrome Publishing appreciates the support, help, and encouragement received from Lia Lauryn Chan; Tiana Chan; Dr. Shu Bong Chan; Soo-Young Chin; Ramona I.T. Chun; Naomi Hirahara; Marla V. Hillery; Michael and Kay Janis; Daphne Kwok; Rose Leung; the Organization of Chinese Americans; Dr. Yvonne M. Lau; Dr. Laura Uba; Jeanne Wang; Mitchell and Laura Witkowski; Christie Yamada; Michael Yamada; Tommy Yamada; and George and Vicki Yamate. Without them, this book would not have been possible.

About Polychrome Publishing

Founded in 1990, Polychrome Publishing Corporation is an independent press located in Chicago, Illinois, producing children's books for a multicultural market. Polychrome books introduce characters and illustrate situations with which children of all colors can identify. They are designed to promote racial, ethnic, cultural, and religious tolerance and understanding. We live in a multicultural world. We at Polychrome Publishing believe that our children need a balanced multicultural education if they are to thrive in that world. Polychrome books can help create that balance.

Other Books by Polychrome Publishing

Almond Cookies & Dragon Well Tea

ISBN #1-879965-03-8
by Cynthia Chin-Lee; illustrations by You Shan Tang. Erica, an European American girl, visits the home of Nancy, her Chinese American friend. In her glimpse of Nancy's cultural heritage, Erica finds much to admire and enjoy. In introducing Erica to her family's culture, Nancy discovers that she needn't feel embarrassed or ashamed about it. Together, the two girls learn that the more they share, the more each of them has. 36 pages, hardbound with paper jacket; full color illustrations. "Well crafted. Very stylish for today's America."—The Book Reader.

Ashok By Any Other Name

ISBN #1-879965-01-1
by Sandra S. Yamate; illustrations by Janice Tohinaka. Ashok is an Indian American boy who wishes he had a more "American" name. In a series of mishaps, he searches for the perfect name for himself. A story for every immigrant or child of immigrants who struggles to be an American. 36 pages, hardbound with paper jacket; full color illustrations. "The book is well-written and would make an excellent addition to a primary school library." —India West.

Bon Odori Dancer

ISBN #1-879965-18-6
by Karen Kawamoto McCoy; illustrations by Carolina Yao. Poor Keiko! Obon is just a few weeks away but she is the clumsiest girl in her dance class. Will she ever be able to learn the traditional dance steps in time? 32 pages, hardbound with paper jacket; full color illustrations and a diagram of dance steps to learn at home.

Blue Jay In The Desert

ISBN #1-879965-04-6
by Marlene Shigekawa; illustrations by Isao Kikuchi.
The story of a Japanese American boy and his family
interned during World War II. Junior doesn't quite
understand what the internment is all about but through
his eyes we see how it has affected the adults around
him. Fortunately, Junior has Grandfather, from whom he
receives a special message of hope. A picture book
introducing the history of the Japanese American internment. 36 pages, hardbound with paper jacket; full color
illustrations. Showcased by Teaching Tolerance Magazine.

Char Siu Bao Boy

ISBN #1-879965-19-4
by Sandra S. Yamate; illustrations by Carolina Yao.
Charlie likes char siu bar (barbecued pork buns) but the
kids at school think they're terrible. Should Charlie make
his friends happy by conforming? A warm-hearted story
about peer pressure and the benefits of sharing one's
cultural heritage. 32 pages, hardbound with paper jacket;
full color illustrations.

Children of Asian America

ISBN #1-879965-15-1
compiled on behalf of the Asian American Coalition.
An anthology exploring childhood from 10 Asian ethnic
communities: Bangladeshi, Cambodian, Chinese, Filipino,
Indian, Japanese, Korean, Laotian, Pakistani, Thai,
Vietnamese, plus bi-racial and pan-Asian American. 120
pages, hardbound with paper jacket; with photographs by
Gene H. Mayeda. Named Pick of the Lists. "This is a book
for all Asian Americans and their friends. . . [and] can
help all of us deal with the complex identity of being
Asian American. . . . an engaging piece of literature,
punctuated throughout with captivating photos."
—Northwest Asian Weekly.

Chopsticks From America

ISBN #1-879965-11-9
by Elaine Hosozawa-Nagano;
illustrations by Masayuki Miyata.
When two Japanese American children go to Japan, they learn that the country of their forebears is not what they expected. But before long, the unfamiliar becomes familiar, expanding to tolerance and acceptance of differences. It's part of growing up. 64 pages, hardbound with paper jacket; full color illustrations and a glossary. A Parent Council Choice Book. Recommended by the Children's Book Review and Midwest Bookwatch.

The Lobster and The Sea

ISBN #1-879965-14-3
by Esther Chiu; illustrations by Mika Takahashi.
A child reconciles her American values with her Grandfather's Asian ones when he decides it is time, as the Chinese say, to return to his roots. A tale to reassure any child faced with the imminent departure of a loved one that separation will not undermine the infinite nature of love. 32 pages, hardbound with paper jacket; full color illustrations.

Nikkei Donburi:
A Japanese American Cultural Survival Guide

ISBN #1-879965-18-6
by Chris Aihara w/ The Japanese American Cultural & Community Center.
Explore Japanese American culture season by season through stories, pictures, and arts & crafts. Includes recipes, patterns for projects, and historical context. Perfect for families or teachers. 124 pages, soft cover.

Pop'n Kimchi

ISBN #1-879965-17-8

by Soo-Young Chin and Christina Lochmann.
w/ The Korean American Museum.

A rhyming pop-up book for all ages about everyone's favorite pickled cabbage! Part of the Kimchi Extravaganza Exhibit! Fun, lively, and informative! Will leave you with a taste for kimchi and rice!

One Small Girl

ISBN #1-879965-05-4

by Jennifer L. Chan; illustrations by Wendy K. Lee.

Jennifer is one small girl trying to amuse herself. Going back and forth between two stores, Jennifer finds a way to double the entertainment for one small girl. A rhythmic and whimsical tale about a small girl's fun fooling big grown-ups. 30 pages, hardbound with paper jacket; full color illustrations. "Kids will delight in the sound effects of shoes clicking on store floors and a small girl's discovery of personal power."—Children's Bookwatch.

Stella: On The Edge Of Popularity

ISBN #1-879965-08-9
by Lauren Lee.

Stella, a Korean American pre-teen, is caught between two cultures. At home, she must be a good Korean girl, but at school, Stella is American, aching to be popular and fit in. Can she balance cultural values and peer pressure . . . and still be herself? A realistic story with which any 1.5 or 2nd generation American will readily identify. 184 pages, hardbound with paper jacket. "Well-developed characters and a credible plot will hold the interest of readers."—School Library Journal. "An excellent job of detailing the identity conflicts of young Korean American girls."—Asian Week. "A must-read for parents and their children."—Korea Central Daily News.

Thanksgiving At Obaachan's

ISBN #1-879965-07-0
by Janet Mitsui Brown.
A Japanese American girl describes how Obaachan
(Grandmother) makes Thanksgiving special. Anyone
whose family has expanded this traditional American
holiday to include their cultural heritage will appreciate
this story and treasure the memories it evokes. 36 pages,
hardbound with paper jacket; full color illustrations and a
glossary. Named Pick of the Lists; A Parent Council Selection.
"Warm, intergenerational and reminiscent of life with
grandmother . . . a family story, beautifully illustrated,
lovingly told."– American Bookseller. "The quintessential
Sansei story." –San Francisco Examiner.